The Ant's Pants

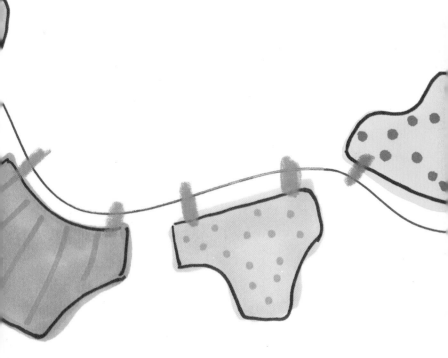

There are lots of Early Reader
stories you might enjoy.

For a complete list, visit
www.hachettechildrens.co.uk

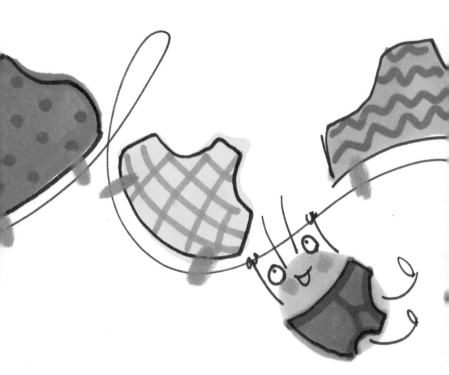

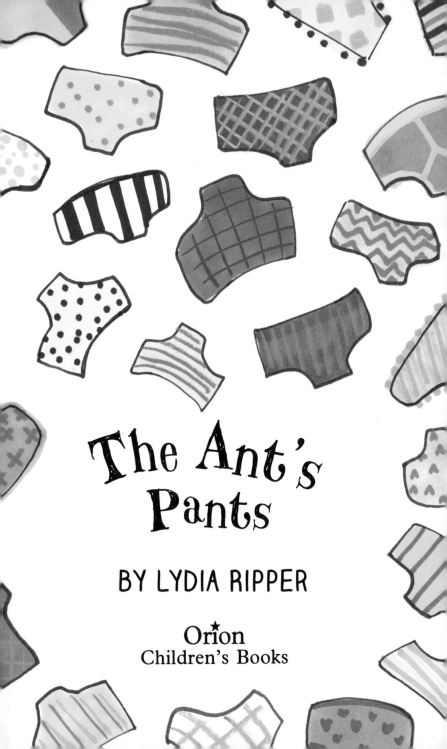

The Ant's Pants

BY LYDIA RIPPER

Orion
Children's Books

ORION CHILDREN'S BOOKS

First published in Great Britain in 2018
by Hodder and Stoughton

1 3 5 7 9 10 8 6 4 2

A CIP catalogue record for this book
is available from the British Library.

ISBN 978 1 5101 0183 8

Printed and bound in China

The paper and board used in this book are from well-managed forests
and other responsible sources.

Orion Children's Books
An imprint of
Hachette Children's Group
Part of Hodder and Stoughton
Carmelite House
50 Victoria Embankment
London EC4Y 0DZ

An Hachette UK Company
www.hachette.co.uk

www.hachettechildrens.co.uk

For my beautiful cousin Georgina

Contents

Chapter One
The Pants Family

These are a pair of pants.
Obviously.

But they are not
ordinary pants.

Inside these pants lives a tiny
little ant called Scaredy Pants.

'Hello!'

Instead of
wearing his pants,
he hides inside them
because he is a BIG
scaredy ant.

Scaredy Pants is part
of a family of ants, called
the Pants.

They live deep underground. Every morning they gather together to feast on a delicious stack of pantcakes.

Mr Fancy Pants is stylish, quirky and owns the most fabulous pants in town.

Mrs Smarty Pants is clever, quick and is always scribbling down genius ideas.

Miss Bossy Pants is Scaredy's older sister. She happily orders everyone about, however big or small.

Little Smelly Pants is the youngest. She lives up to her name. Wherever she goes a stinky pong follows.

Boxer is the mischievous family pet. He's a bug, but even he wears pants!

And finally there's Scaredy
Pants. He's scared of . . .

EVERYTHING!

Creepy crawlies
chilled him . . .

the tooth fairy
freaked him . . .

the vacuum
cleaner panicked
him . . .

thunderstorms
startled him . . .

AND the idea of monsters
spooked him …

Aaaaaaaaahhhhhhhh!

But Scaredy was sad. He wanted to be brave like the super ants in his favourite comic books.

'Scaredy needs a little courage!' said Mrs Smarty Pants.

'He just needs to practice. I have a pant-astic idea!' said Mr Fancy Pants.

Chapter Two
Creepy-crawlies

The next day, Mr Fancy Pants set Scaredy the brave task of going out into the garden alone to say hello to a bug.

'But I'm scared of creepy crawlies!'
said Scaredy Pants.

He disliked the giant ones,

the hairy ones,

the spiky ones,

the slimy
ones,

and even the
tiny ones.

WHAAAAAAAAAA!

'If you face your fears, you won't be scared anymore,' said Mr Fancy Pants.

Scaredy Pants took a deep breath, and peeked out of his pants. But the bugs looked huge!

'NOOOOOOO!' he wailed, 'I can't!'

Mr Fancy Pants needed to think of something else, and quick.

He had a very fancy idea indeed . . .

Scaredy started laughing. The bugs were all dressed up. They looked just like his dad!

'Maybe they aren't so scary,' giggled Scaredy.

He took one little step out of his pants.

Mr Fancy Pants felt proud. He gave Scaredy a hug and smiled.

Chapter Three
Thunderstorms

BUT THEN it started raining. Scaredy Pants ran right back inside! Thunderstorms were one of his scariest things.

'Mum, I'm scared!' cried
Scaredy Pants.
    Scaredy hid away from
the thunder . . .

and ducked from
the sudden flashes
of lightning . . .

39

Maybe if Scaredy knows more about storms, he won't be so scared, Mrs Smarty Pants thought. So she taught him that counting between the lighting and thunder would tell him how far away the storm was.

Even though the storm sounded close, it was actually miles away!

WOOOOOOW thought Scaredy,
as he peered out of his pants.

'But the best thing about
a storm is . . .

. . . a den!' said Mrs Smarty Pants.

Scaredy felt safe in the cosy
den. He took another little step
out of his pants . . . to grab three
giant marshmallows . . . YUM!

Mrs Pants cheered and gave him a little squeeze. Scaredy DEFINITELY felt braver.

Chapter Four
Monsters

Once the storm passed, it was bedtime.

But Scaredy was scared of the pant-stealing monsters that lived under his bed.

'I can't sleep!' said Scaredy Pants.

He was sure that the monsters would steal his pants. Every night when the big light went out and Scaredy's little night light came on, he thought he could see monster shadows creeping around the room.

Scaredy tried to
forget about his fears by
reading the heroic tales
of his favourite super
ants, but it didn't work.

His big sister, Bossy Pants,
wasn't afraid of anything.
'What are monsters scared of?'
shouted Bossy Pants . . .
'BIGGER
        MONSTERS!'

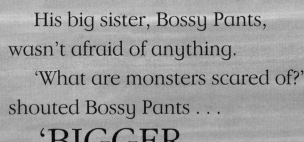

With her monster
costume on, Bossy dived
under Scaredy's bed to frighten
the monsters away . . .

But under the bed there was
only one of Smelly Pants' stinky
nappies, an old teddy bear and a
wrinkled sleeping bag!

'There's nothing to be scared
of!' giggled Bossy.

She squished the teddy bear,
threw the nappy across the floor
and wrestled with the sleeping bag.

'There, the monsters are all
gone,' said Bossy.

'Wow! You're so brave,' said
Scaredy.
'Will you go to sleep now?'
asked Bossy Pants.

'What if the monsters come back?' whispered Scaredy, as he peeked out from his pants.

So Bossy had another idea.

'We'll have a sleepover!' she shrieked. 'I'll sleep in your room tonight!'

With Bossy by his side, Scaredy felt almost brave enough to sleep like a normal ant . . .

Chapter Five
Washday

Despite his family's efforts,
Scaredy still spent most of his
time hiding in his pants. Until . . .

'WASHDAY!' shouted Mrs
Smarty Pants.

'Oh no!' cried Scaredy Pants.
Washday was the one day
where everyone had to put their
pants in the washing machine.

*What can I hide under? I
don't have a spare pair of pants,*
thought Scaredy Pants. He had
always been too afraid to pick a
second pair.

When it came to wash o'clock the family couldn't find Scaredy Pants. They looked under things, over things, between things.

'Oh Scaredy, where are you?'
called the Pants family.

But Scaredy was nowhere to
be seen.

'We can't start the wash
without Scaredy's pants!' said Mr
Fancy Pants.

The family went off on a hunt, leaving Boxer and Smelly Pants alone with the washing machine.

WHOOSH, CLICK, FLICK, BANG, BEEP ... the washing machine was alive!

But Boxer had used far too much powder and the washing machine was NOT happy.

Boxer ran
for his life as
the washing
machine spat bubbles,

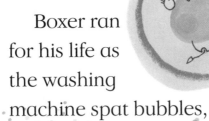

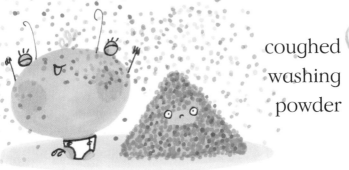

coughed
washing
powder

and grew bigger and bigger . . .
'It's going to explode!' barked
Boxer.

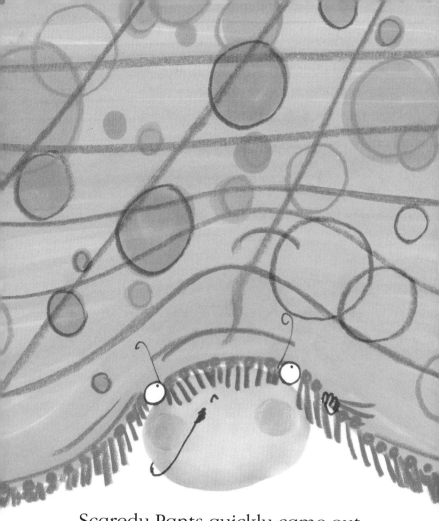

Scaredy Pants quickly came out
of his hiding place under the rug.

*I must help save little Smelly
Pants!* thought Scaredy. *She can't
be trapped in a sea of bubbles.*

Scaredy turned his pants into a cape and was now SUPER PANTS the flying ant. And Super Pants was afraid of NOTHING . . .

His family got back just in time to see Scaredy save his little sister!

But with all the excitement,
Super Pants had forgotten one very
important thing . . .

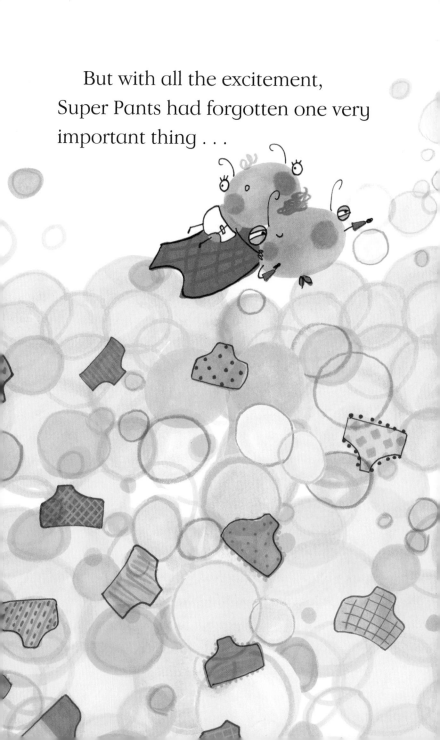

. . . to wear any pants at all!